Vincent

CHEECH
AND THE SPOOKY GHOST BUS

by Cheech Marin
illustrated by Orlando L. Ramírez

HarperCollinsPublishers

GOOD MORNING!

My name is Cheech, and I'll be your school bus driver today. I am a really really really REALLY good bus driver. I always get to school on time, and I always take my Cheecharrones on the best field trips.

Well, ALMOST always.

Once, when I was driving through a scary graveyard, I noticed some kids waiting at a bus stop. They looked sort of weird, but the first rule of bus driving is that you pick up all the kids at the bus stop, even the weird-looking ones.

But when I opened the bus door, the kids were gone!

After that, I noticed the Cheecharrones screaming and shouting more than usual. At first I figured they were just having fun. And I had to keep my eyes on the road! Then they told me the bus was haunted.

"There's no such thing as ghosts," I said.
"I haven't believed in ghosts since I was a little kid."
Then I turned around.

First we tried to scare them away.

They **weren't** SCARED.

Then we played a song called
"Ghosts, Go Home."

The ghosts just clapped and sang a song called
"Ghosts Are Here to Stay"!

Then
we tried
to chase
them
away.

"GHOSTS ARE FUN!"

the Cheecharrones shouted.

The ghosts *did* look fun. *Everyone* was having fun. So much fun that they forgot all about me.

I had to get rid of those ghosts!

"No ghosts allowed!" I said. "That's bus rule number five!"
"Are you serious?" Carmen asked. "Is that a real rule?"
"Sorry," I said. "But all ghosts have to leave the bus!"

That was much easier than I expected.
But the ghosts hadn't gone far!

The ghosts flew us through a ghost town. Then they landed in front of a ghost school!

That was too much! Those ghosts had no respect for the bus rules. I was about to give a lecture about bus safety when I felt a tap on my shoulder. . . .

A ghost bus driver!
"You found my ghostitos!" the ghost driver said.
And he gave me a big ghost hug!

Now I had a ghost friend of my own! And he was a bus driver. Bus drivers make great friends.

And it was all because of those crazy ghosts!